*To Jay and Jonah Northern,
with love*

Copyright 2020 by Teasa Northern. All rights reserved. No part of this book may be reproduced or transmitted in any form or by any means, electronic or mechanical, including photocopying, recording, or by any information storage and retrival system without written permission of the author.

Scripture quotations marked (NLT) are taken from the Holy Bible, New Living Translation, copyright 1996, 2004, 2015 by Tyndale House Foundation. Used by permission of Tyndale House Publishers, a Division of Tyndale House Ministries, Carol Stream, Illinois 60188. All rights reserved.

Edited by Sophia Williams and Jillian Northern

Ellie and the Swans

By Teasa Northern with Jillian Northern

Illustrated by Ryan Ferrell

For **all** the little **Ellies** in the world....

Once upon a time, there was a **little eagle** named **Ellie**. She lived among a family of swans.

Her **beak** was **hooked** and **pointy**.
Her **eyes** were **big** and **sharp**.
Her **feet** were **claw-like**
and **not good** for swimming.

As much as **Ellie tried** to look and act like them, **it was impossible.**

The swans always seemed to be able to do things that Ellie could not do.

She tried her very best to swim gracefully, but her feet **would not glide across the water.**

Once the others noticed **Ellie was different** they began to tease her.

They made fun of her **eyes** and **beak**.
They laughed at her **long wings** and giggled when **she struggled to swim** in the water.

Little Ellie became **discouraged** by their words. She spent a lot of time **alone**, away from the swans who no longer wanted to play with her.

One day, as Ellie played quietly by herself, the **Lord** came and began to speak to her.

"Oh, my little eagle, don't you know that **you** are **perfectly made?**"

"When **I** made you, **I** had a **special plan.**"

As Ellie listened, the Lord explained.

"Your wings are long so you can soar high in the air."

"Your eyes help you see your prey from a great distance."

"Your **feet** were made to **move swiftly**."

"Your **beak** is extremely **strong and powerful**."

Ellie went excitedly to her family of swans and told them what the Lord had shared.

She explained to them **all of the things she could do**. But the swans didn't believe **Ellie**, and laughed at her once again.

The Lord came to Ellie once more.
This time He said,
"It's time to soar in the air Ellie."

But Ellie's heart was filled with uncertainty. Her family didn't believe she could do it, and now she wasn't sure she could either.

The Lord asked her, "Do you trust me? Can you trust me with all of your heart even if you don't understand?"

Ellie sat and **thought** about this for a while.

If **He** said she was **meant to soar high** and **do great things**, she would believe Him.

She decided to **be the eagle** she was **meant to be.**

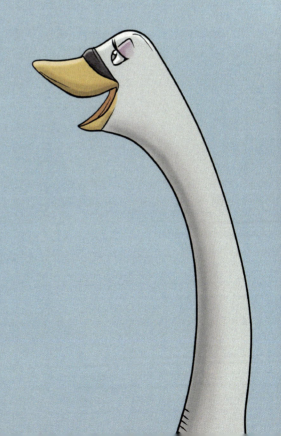

Those who **trust** in the **Lord** will find **new strength.**
They will **soar high on wings** like eagles.
They will **run** and **not grow weary.**
They will **walk** and **not faint.**

Isaiah 40:31 NLT

Made in the USA
Monee, IL
04 December 2021

82930274R00021